Evenings & Avenues

ALSO BY STUART DISCHELL

Good Hope Road

EVENINGS & AVENUES

Stuart Dischell

Stuart Dischell (signature)

5. 1. 01

 PENGUIN POETS

PENGUIN BOOKS
Published by the Penguin Group
Penguin Books USA Inc., 375 Hudson Street, New York, New York 10014, U.S.A.
Penguin Books Ltd, 27 Wrights Lane, London W8 5TZ, England
Penguin Books Australia Ltd, Ringwood, Victoria, Australia
Penguin Books Canada Ltd, 10 Alcorn Avenue, Toronto, Ontario, Canada M4V 3B2
Penguin Books (N.Z.) Ltd, 182–190 Wairau Road, Auckland 10, New Zealand

Penguin Books Ltd, Registered Offices: Harmondsworth, Middlesex, England

First published in Penguin Books 1996

10 9 8 7 6 5 4 3 2 1

LIBRARY OF CONGRESS CATALOGING IN PUBLICATION DATA
Dischell, Stuart.
    Evenings & avenues / Stuart Dischell.
       p   cm.
    ISBN 0 14 05.8766 7
    I. Title.
PS3554.I827E94   1996
811'.54—dc20   96-6279

Printed in the United States of America
Set in Janson
Designed by Brian Mulligan

FOR CAROLINE MARINA DISCHELL

*For Peter Stitt —
w/ friendship &
remembrance of the courts
& tables of Palm Springs —
Best,
Stuart*

. . . century of clouds

　　—Apollinaire, *Phantom of the Clouds*

ACKNOWLEDGMENTS AND NOTES

Grateful acknowledgment is made to the following publications in which certain of the poems in *Evenings & Avenues* first appeared: *AGNI* ("Ellipsis, Third or Fourth Dot, Depending," "Evening," and "People Who Talk to Themselves"); *Alaska Quarterly Review* ("In Daylight" and "The Spider"); *Boston Review* ("Evening III"); *Boulevard* ("Evening VI"); *Colorado Review* ("An Account" and "An Arrangement"); *Harvard Review* (" 'The Girls in Their Summer Dresses, Take II' "); *The New Republic* ("The Foreign Correspondent"); *The Notre Dame Review* ("Evening V" and "The Rockpile"); *Partisan Review* ("Several Dioramas, Some Invented, Some Remembered, from the Musée Grevin"); *Ploughshares* ("End of the Century," "Evening II," "Psalm," and "The Talking Cure"); *Puerto del Sol* ("The Bachelor," "Morning by the Sea," "The Point," "The Resort," and "Skylight Travel"); and *Stuff* ("A Living"). "The Yellow Slicker" was printed as a broadside by Fecundity Press, Greensboro, North Carolina.

"The Foreign Correspondent": for James Preston O'Donnell (1918–1990). The last line is my misquotation of Bertolt Brecht's *Galileo*. *Andrea (in the door): Unhappy is the land that breeds no hero. Galileo: No, Andrea, unhappy is the land that needs a hero.* " 'The Girls in Their Summer Dresses, Take II' ": homage to Irwin Shaw. "End of the Century": *She stretched her young body and went out* is a variation of what Grete does at the end of Kafka's *Metamorphosis*. "Street Piece": was suggested by Cesare Pavese's *The drunk leaves ruined houses in his wake*. "Speaking Parts": for Tom Sleigh, based upon something he accused me of. "Psalm": homage to Edwin Muir. My thanks to my brother, Mark, to the friends who advised this book in manuscript, and to Dawn Drzal.

Contents

Ellipsis, Third or Fourth Dot, Depending   1

Dustpan and Broom   4

Evening   5

Morning by the Sea   7

Explorations   8

A Saint's Life   9

The Foreign Correspondent   11

Evening II   13

The Bachelor   14

The Spider   15

In Camera   16

An Affair   17

"The Girls in Their Summer Dresses, Take II"   19

Evening III   21

Skylight Travel   22

The Resort   23

The Cove   24

The Yellow Slicker   25

End of the Century   26

A Living   28

Evening IV   29

People Who Talk to Themselves   30

Street Piece   32

In Daylight   33

The Talking Cure   35

The Two   37

Hours in the Sky   38

Among Fisherfolk   39

The Point   40

The Rockpile   41

Evening V   42

Volume   43

Speaking Parts   45

Return Address   46

Inspiriter   47

Evening VI   55

In Cases Like These   56

An Account   58

An Arrangement   60

The Edifice   62

Gates of the City   64

Evening VII   65

Psalm   67

Several Dioramas, Some Remembered, Some Invented,
    from the Musée Grevin   68

Evenings & Avenues

ELLIPSIS, THIRD OR
FOURTH DOT, DEPENDING

"All my life I wanted to join the carnival.
I would be happy there upon the midway,
Tearing the heads off chickens. I know
This sounds grotesque, someone's mad ravings
Or sick bravado. How to say, I mean it only
Metaphorically. When I compare myself
I don't appear so badly. The mess I have
Made around me, which is not chicken heads
But letters, library books, shut-off notices,
Rebukes me less. I see myself as a defined
Person, one with sharp edges, a good suit
That fits and a silk shirt buttoned to the neck.
The world loves a gent. It looks at my shoes.
I wear a white scarf and I am off to the opera.
All my life I wanted to join the opera.
I would be perfect there among the painted sets,
Singing basso profundo under my cap. I could
Even play a woman there and show the crowd
Things I am capable of doing. The flowers thrown
To the footlights would enclose me like a garden.
All my life I wanted to exist in a garden.
Standing like a timepiece in the center of the lawn,
The barely perceptible movement of my shadow

Would be nonetheless significant as the hours
That revolve on my face. At night I'd be meaning-
Less to anyone but myself, or on a cloudy day.
All my life I wanted to join the clouds,
To be among them, the easily ethereal,
The ever-changing, and handsomely made. I
Would drift, congregate, vanish, roll in,
And sometimes touch the others into a day
So black the ground seems farther than the sky.
All my life I wanted to be the sky,
To carry the whole of the world inside me,
To pat my forests and deserts with satisfaction.
My God, I could be the child Sky Day,
Born on a commune to idealists, given to
Wearing black and nose rings and being twenty
For the first and only time in his/her life;
To be that shaven-headed and vital, to have
Written in paint on the wall of the city
When all my life I wanted to be that wall—
Part of the neighborhood, the block, the building:
To be seen in a rush through the express bus window
Or studied a long time in traffic. HOW MANY
DEAD, MR. PRESIDENT. NO BLOOD FOR OIL.
DANIELLE I STILL LOVE YOU. ICE RULES.
And I have wanted to be my neighborhood,
My block, my building. I have wanted

To be this city where I live, to walk down
The avenues of myself, whistling a tune
Through all the people that look like me."

DUSTPAN AND BROOM

Broom believes that movement is best,
The one who stops gets thrown out.
Perhaps she remembers her earthly roots,
The woodsman's ax, the farmer's scythe.

Dustpan is the laziest of fellows,
Lying on floors or leaning on walls.
He would leave all matter in corners.
Being of plastic, he will stay forever.

Dustpan and broom, a handsome pair,
Mismatched in height but suited for work.
Broom so willing, attentive, at hand.
Dustpan hiding, shirking his share.

EVENING

For an hour or two the evening has no limits
Or so it seems to you as you walk the pavements
Of this, your adoptive city. Before you the sun
At play lights the windows of the office buildings
In the vault of the avenue, conveying odd images
Like the faces seen in the flames of the hearth.

For an hour or two the evening has no limits
And you are pedaling again your English Racer,
Riding double down the boardwalk along the sea,
Your girlfriend sideways on the bar, her legs
Dangling out of the way, the wind blowing the ironed
Length of her hair, the wind covering and revealing
The profile of her face. Her young body was snug
Between your arms when you steered the handlebars
Past all the frowning strollers. For awhile you forget
But always it comes back, your brother's cologne
You wore, the games you played on her parents' bed
Until the headlights on the wall drove you home
Naked inside your clothes. She is a mother now,
You suppose. It happens that people lose touch.

The evening has no limits and the streets go on
What could be forever, linking cities and outposts;

Suburbs that were villages separated by farms
Have merged the way they once were forested.
What it means to be alive has never troubled you.
Strange as you are you have always felt this welcome.

MORNING BY THE SEA

The atrocities of the last world war
Mean little at the moment she smooths
Her blanket on the shore. First to the beach,
She claims the high ground, near the rocks
Where the surf has scooped out a small bluff.
The morning is breezeless but nonetheless
She anchors the blanket with her clogs and bag,
And for the last corner the historical novel
She has carried all summer for its purpose.

Behind fences and porches, in the pastel houses,
The pale food of morning is served at the table.
Insistent parents and their willful children
Push back and forth the calm air of morning.
Above their heads the ceiling fan turns,
Five blades in the air flipping the pages
Of news and recipes and advice for the future.

EXPLORATIONS

Those overseas places with mysterious names
Have possessed him since the earliest times
He saw them pasted in his brother's collection,
Or spun so fast on the turning globe
He believed they might fall off the world.

Then, grown, a man, he sought them out,
Leaving one land for another, packing a bag
With the plans of cities. A genius of arrivals
And departures, he figured the best ways to travel—
Air, land, or sea, in or out of season.

It's the staying that has brought him trouble,
The building of others' expectations, neighbors
And bosses, lovers who thought he'd keep till
Morning. Now something more odd is happening,
As if the present is the past repeating, and

The glory of the future has become a haze of names,
Like the ones he slept with and remembers indistinctly,
Not as persons but as experiences more general,
Something that occurred to his body. No place
On earth could be foreign to him whose name is legion.

A SAINT'S LIFE

The last guest at the party
Still up for it
After twenty years of parties,
Like a mockingbird you sang
The songs the others sang,
Like a mockingbird
Your singing pleased you.

And the tumblers of whisky,
Sour Mash or Scotch
And the beautiful beer bottles
Green or brown or clear
Fanned out and closed like a target
On the rug where you passed out.

It was the "war of nerves"
Or "just a mood"
Made you swallow, a sadness
You steered away from and toward
With delight, like a ship
On a round the world cruise.

I would not want to be that body
The earth will meet too soon,

Or the poor soul you exhaled,
Puffing him out like smoke,
Yet one night in this dream,
Cast off in a boat,
I sailed around in circles
Until I found you waiting,
Laughing head tilted back,
Well lit, your mother's son,
The drunken face of God.

THE FOREIGN CORRESPONDENT

Debts, war medals, a regiment of dry
Cleaner bags of suits in the closet,
The finest European tailors circa
The Cold War, your glorious tuxedo
Supervising the digging of Berlin
Tunnels or meetings with the President—

His brother, Joe, a friend before
Harvard and The War, fellow skinny
Dippers caught by the cops off Marshfield
And later by death, yours last. The attendants
Were suitably grim, the gurney wheels
Quiet in the length of the dormitory hall.

Glad to meet the youthful scholars,
Hitler was ebullient, poured the drinks.
An invitation to the embassy. You wrote
A book on Yeats, prompted by your mentor,
Robert Hillyer. Eight years later,
Walking through the Fuehrer Bunker rubble

You saw the center had in fact held.
You knew the enemy so well, most times
You looked the part—elegant, spy-cultured

By the O.S.S. and Operation Paperclip,
Mixing it up with left wing artists,
Spiriting Nazi scientists to America.

You inspired uprisings and misinformation,
The popular fare of *The Saturday Evening Post*
Articles you knocked out on your Remington.
You got on well with Camus and Brecht,
Had a pretty wife that slept with both,
As you charted the regions of your borderless state.

"Blessed is the land that needs no heroes."

EVENING II

Morning let you down like a broken promise.
Noon with its bright clothes stood in your way.
Now it is evening, though, your favorite time,
The kiss of the word feeling good in your mouth.

It is sad to think of people you have failed,
Who thought, early on, you lived up to your word,
Who learned their lesson in bed, at play, or at work.
You were only yourself. You promised them nothing.

Perhaps it was death you were hoping to miss,
Like a pothole or slick in the road at night, the human
Complication that comes with being or being with.
Better a crow or a mutt or the ground you stand on.

But you are not evil on the pavement this evening,
And those you harmed have gotten over you fine.
Improved, in fact, by the wake of your departure,
They do better than you could ever imagine.

THE BACHELOR

Single again he rents a studio apartment,
But in the evening with a glass of wine he is married.
At home with his wife he had dreams of bright young women.
For hours they would make love to him, and then
They would talk about books he loved as a single man.

This is how you think it will be, this life invented
With another close by, that the summer will bring you back
Muscled, lean, tan, that you will ride again
The rollers on a waxed board and the tips of your hair
Will be blond in the honeyed permanence of the afternoon.

Single again he swirls the cold wine.
The yellow tinted, transparent, fermented liquid
Tastes of peaches, of butter, of oak. The few
Flecks of cork remind him of the life he has saved.
But the aftertaste on the tongue is chemical and peculiar.

THE SPIDER

All that time near the radiator in winter
Or the open window of summer, you wrote
The chapters instead of living them.
What did you know? That the 77 Bus
Passed your corner three times an hour,
That men but never women relieved themselves
In the alley behind the pharmacy, that the trees'
Seasonal arrangements were no more than a detail,
An off-centerpiece at the great buffet.

Easy to laugh at the endeavors of others,
Their historic-comic-tragic misadventures.
Slapstick, black and white, sped-up stickfigures,
They walked out of marriages, capered through jobs.
Their occupations were always artists and models,
People down on their luck and living downtown.
No one ever worked the regular hours or held
The professions, your pets of corruption.

You grew old there below the rafters,
All those years believing you were the spider,
But you were merely the web,
Attracting what life you could.

IN CAMERA

She asked my opinion of some photos she had taken
Of herself with a time-delay shutter.
Several were immodest and one, in fact, erotic.
She was the true blondest of all descended angels.

Some mornings, pupils wide with mescaline,
She dropped by my apartment. Twenty years ago
And still I picture her naked ageless legs
Parted on a bed, not mine, her face turned discretely away, oh.

AN AFFAIR

I

They met early in the morning while his girlfriend
Was sleeping, when he said he went to the studio
To get to work early, or the days when his girlfriend worked.
Just an hour or two in the morning for sex.

II

What she got out of it is difficult to say.
Interfered-with, temporarily futureless,
She lived in the present. Unsentimental,
She kept nothing he gave her.

III

It was clear she waited for someone
To move her. The safe-sexual fondling
Encouraged her, engorged her fantasies of
Bodily contractions not erotic detours.

IV

Kisses like bees, she stopped calling
Him the honey-bear endearments
Of the silly in bed. After sex
She once slapped his face.

"THE GIRLS IN THEIR SUMMER DRESSES, TAKE II"

He had hurt her as he always did,
Unintentionally, these Sunday afternoons,
After their morning of struggling over what to do—
They had risen late and going back to bed
Would kill the day. Imagine him thinking that
Twenty years ago, but now he had said it
And she looked out the window, saying with her eyes,
"If we don't have each other, we still have the world."

Outside on the streets, empty of cars and trucks,
The occasional cab rolled unhailed down Fifth Avenue,
For who would not walk this perfect August day,
Dry, unseasonable, with a little Autumn breeze
To tug at the hems of the girls in their summer dresses.
Yes, he saw them as soon as he left the apartment,
And she knew right away why it was he looked back.
"Please, don't be so obvious," she wanted to tell him,
Then hurried the pace on their walk to the park.

The future seemed dim to her now and the past
She recalled only as this morning when she sat
Idly in the big chair in her underpants and bra,
Slowly turning the pages of *The Times* to see what

He would do. Even now, sitting on the bench together,
His eyes moved away from her towards the girl,
Not even pretty, walking past them in gauzy cotton.
The sun tracing between her slender thighs,
The sun shining its otherwise painful summer light.

EVENING III

In another country beside a sea far calmer
Than our own, I watched the evening begin
On the mountain, ease itself down the slopes
Of lavender, and stretch full out on the water.

To me it happened so quickly, but it was just
The evening taking its time. To the evening all
Acts of exertion are fruitless, a farce of human
Proportion. The evening knows what's really important.

The evening likes wine and the bathers who strip
Their suits and hang them from the terrace rail.
The evening likes cheese and olives and things that give
Themselves up with little effort. The evening likes slow

Sex, to play with the toes, the knees, the hips
Of the lovers. To climb the ribs of their torsos
And reveal to each their unkissed places. To
Astonish them with their illuminated faces.

SKYLIGHT TRAVEL

She observes the posters and brochures
That inform her every idle look that life
Elsewhere is a continuous option, a carpet
Rolled out beyond the horizon where the single
Appear profound, not lonely, as they stare over
The sea wall at a ship or upon a plate of shrimp.

Life elsewhere has a firm stomach, wears shorts
In the winter, has hair just the right color.
Every towel is fresh as in the best hotels.
And the bed is a masterpiece, a triumph of taste,
Brass or wood. There she will be able
To be the person that nobody has yet seen.

Above her head the quality of the sun
At the end of the day is muted by the not
Entirely clear arc of the skylight:
Plexiglas, created to conform to the odd
Angles of rooftops, the wind, the rain,
And all the known possibilities of weather.

THE RESORT

Through the table, an umbrella.
Upon the umbrella, a name,
Some beverage with a bright color
And bitter taste. The couple
Sits impossibly quiet, listening
For the explosions on the sun.

I had a thought and then I lost it.
It would be best to stay this way forever,
A man and a woman at a small white table
On a perfectly clear afternoon.
He enjoys his shirt with its sporty logo.
She is glad she wore the straw hat.

It is forty feet back to the hotel.
One street to cross and two flights up.
Half a turn in the lock and the door opens
To a bed, two water glasses, and a clock.
The carpet measures one quarter inch thick,
Impressed with wet heels from the bath.

I should let them run and take their clothes off.
Let them repair what they have left of their lives.
But it is not yet the time to release them.
I may keep us here all afternoon.

THE COVE

The trees do not move all day.
They do not move forever.

And the bathers in their dark costumes
Will not take their feet out of the water.

How does the bird freeze in flight,
And the meat in the shadows not spoil?

No one is moving now.
Nothing moves ever.

Not thirst. Not heat. Not summer. Not fire.
Not the urge in the loins of the reclining figure,

Or the word on the lips of the speaker.
Unbroken wave. Unblinking eye.

Full moon of the postmark
Below the bent corner.

THE YELLOW SLICKER

On this fourth day in a row of rain
There is a sameness to the streets broken only by the odd
Brightly painted house—the way those who pass by
In tan or black trench coats look back at the girl
Wearing a yellow slicker. The yellow slicker,
A gift from her aunt who knew London would be wet,
Having lived there herself just after The War,
The Europe she had known transformed to a state
Of the mind, no longer Central but Eastern, far away,
Bombed-out, depopulated, at least of her kind.

But for a girl of nineteen with American thoughts,
Traveler's cheques, a boy at home, a university
Address, the decline of the West compels less
Than each step she takes through the London rain.
Even these British so accustomed to their weather
Admire the girl in the yellow slicker, as if she
With her uncovered streaming blond hair might shine
As the only sun they will see all week. Now,
That's the kind of history she likes to hear.

END OF THE CENTURY

I. Displaced Persons

Out on the street the children are playing soldier.
It's the end of the century and still they play soldier.
Let's be unfair. Blame them for the toasted corpses,
The orphans, widows, and amputees. One aims
A broomstick, another a plastic missile launcher,
And the little ones on the lawn roll over, "I'm dead,"
They say with joy, "I'm dead," "I'm dead," "I'm dead."

II. She Stretched Her Young Body and Went Out

She stretched her young body and went out.
The trolley lines were bright in the sun.
Bees hovered on her dress pattern.
The flowers were of spectral colors.

She was still her parents' girl, living home,
Helping out. She was always the one. She believed
In her soul, in birthday parties, in feathers and drums.
She lived in every neighborhood. You saw her.

III. Sarajevo Zoo

With two buckets of water he had gone to the cages.
It was early in the morning, the shelling had stopped.
In a tan windbreaker he had gone to the bears.
He made our target, this old man walking.

A LIVING

Someday I will open a shop
Where I will sell an assortment
Of things I like to have—
Statues of horses, raku vases,
Ovenware made of porcelain,
Sweaters of wool and cotton,
Shoes, mostly slippers, sun-
Glasses, broad-brimmed hats, a trunk
Filled with scarves and silk remnants.
There will be cards and books
With odd titles: "Washington Square
Upside Down on Thursday," or "The Memoir
Of a Foreign Giant." It will be like
A store I saw in North Beach but nothing
Like it really. It will be mine.
I will keep a dog there, an ancient
Shepherd spread in the doorway,
Admiring my customers' ankles
As one by one they step over her.
I won't ever marry. I will fix-
Up a room behind a curtain
And wear the clothes that suit me,
Sometimes changing in the afternoons.

EVENING IV

Walking the long blocks home after work
On my feet I am the child coming from school,
An embarrassing thought the way it means
My wife's my mother and not my daughter's.

Late autumn evening the sun quits early,
The porch lights turn on, and the leaf-
Strewn sidewalks alert family dogs
To your presence along the property lines.

This is good you believe, another proof
Your existence on earth is not wholly imagined,
Like those late night talks in the common room
. . . if I died in the city and nobody saw me.

If I die in the city and nobody claims me,
Let four trash collectors haul away my body,
Leave me rot in the pit at the edge of the city.
Tell them I was born to be great but never born.

PEOPLE WHO TALK
TO THEMSELVES

At first it appears they are eating something
Delicious, chewing open mouthed and excitedly
The morsels of air, richly voweled, whole
Courses of syllables flavored by finger pointings
And broad gestures. Then it becomes less happy:
Jaw clicked and vacant, they turn in reprisal,
Their partners in argument long since departed,
Another betrayal, the conspiracies of clouds.
Sometimes I have seen one after the other, carrying
On their ancient fervent manner. To the cities
They have come. In the country they were hidden
By families and barns and collections of animals.
But here they assemble in parks and on corners,
Offering their opinions, grievances, enthusiasms,
Their limitless orations on topics of race and gender,
Not unlike Shelley's "unacknowledged legislators."

Once at a time of pain and disappointment, I
Saw the sight of myself in a hairdresser's window.
The faces of the clients were pointed with amusement
As one by one they swiveled toward my appearance.
I still recall the glee of the operators, their
Scissors and combs conducting peals of laughter,
And one particular, blue-smocked patron, who mimed

My movements with detailed attention, picking out
The slouch of my shoulder, my hollowed eyes,
The way my left leg had taken to pulling to the right.
He reflected clearly, disturbingly precise,
Those singular motions of my articulation.
I had been addressing the causer of my sorrow,
Reciting her name to the air's transparency;
Revising her presence across my lips and tongue,
My hunger fed the appetites of women and men.

STREET PIECE

When the addict approaches the others make way for him—
Not the way smaller boats yield to the oncoming liner
But how pigeons will fly at the footsteps of a dog.
It's dangerous getting too close to an addict. He might ask
You for money or, if he's well, run off with your bag.

When the merchants see an addict walk by, they follow
A long time from the center of their eyes. Even the bums,
Piss-smelling in their long coats, observe the addict
With disdain and know we like them better for choosing
The bottle and can over the needle and pipe.

To the addict each city block is a game. All faces
Remembered and changeable in the waning glow of the high.
Each step he takes is made with great effort and forgotten.
With a blind man's dark glasses he keeps his dignity.
Yeah, that's right, like the blind man who sees.

IN DAYLIGHT

When I find a pair of underpants on the sidewalk,
Women's or men's, I know there's a story behind them.

If I am sad, I have a sad story that concerns
A woman who sacrificed so hard for her family
She lost so much weight her underpants rolled down
Her legs, and she stepped right out of them, kicked
Them off, not knowing until later, when she rested
On the table at the clinic where she sold her blood,
Why the crowd of donors was looking up her skirt.

But if I am lonely, I tell a lonely story
Of a man who had nothing but the clothes on his back
And a few garments wrapped in a scarf on a stick.
He lost his spare briefs, having come to our city
To find his natural parents after the foster family
Died in the fire he set. They did not pay attention.
Now, without clean underwear, no one will ever love him.

And if I am horny, I think up a horny story
About the couple that met last night at Brann's Pub,
Who would not walk the distance to get at each other.
In consequence, they merged quickly in the recess

Between shops, her back pressed against the glass,
He lifting her a little to get the right angle,
Her panties dropped or discarded in the process.

I head on home, feeling sad, lonely, and horny.
I sense my own boxer shorts struggling to be free,
To rid themselves finally of my hips and buttocks,
To be pulled from my pants like some magician's trick,
To flap in the wind and come to rest on the pavement,
To show for all to see their inexorable statement
About me, their judgment on my life, my flag of surrender.

THE TALKING CURE

He had done what he promised himself he would do—
Kept his mouth shut in the bar—but now driving
The miles to her house he felt the talk rising
Inside him like ardor, the heat of self-love.
But he swore to himself that tonight he would talk
Mostly with his shoulders and eyes, let his best
Features do the work and answer her questions
With phrases like "it happens" or "that's the way
It is sometimes," constructions that would confirm
By the set of his jaw both the knowledge and sorrow
Of human behavior, as though life had tested him
And taught him that saying little says it all.
He kept his promise and let her do the talking:
Ex-husband, ex-boyfriend, parents who thought her wild,
That last word clinching for him the certainty
They would go home together, that tonight he could trade
His talking for sex. He understood that much
About himself, knew the way women looked at him
Funny whenever he told the versions of his life,
How the light that was passion turned to caution
In their eyes, how between them opened an intersection
That should be avoided—tire skids be damned!
Now driving back to her place, he would not slip
Or even sing along with the music on the radio.

He would refrain from telling her she was beautiful
Beside him in the green glow of the dash. Later,
After their seat belts were unbuckled and reeled back,
Jeans unzipped, the patterned sheets turned back,
After kiss and nuzzle and thrust and the many changed
Positions till she rocking on top, palms pressed
Against the cage of his chest and she gasping,
And folding herself upon him, would his moaning
Her name, his calling her both baby and momma,
And his fluid of tears and come and sweat and spit
Soak them both with the high tide of his loneliness,
Then she would hear him and he would turn away and dress.

THE TWO

The two together walk rough seas—
No, it's the street, the sea's inside.
Half a keg of beer in them,
They haven't got their land legs on.

The two have sailed a long time now—
From Holland to the South China Sea,
Or maybe just the route downtown,
Loading at every bar they pass.

The two like couples arm in arm—
But more like tugs against the tide.
Shambling, unshaven, red-faced, tattooed,
Paired like channel markers, warnings, and cries.

HOURS IN THE SKY

Everyday is a funeral. The labeling of boxes
Like the manufacture of coffins—each one hers—
She places on the belt from shipping to loading.
The light of the fluorescent tubes makes everyone deadly.
She would like to get her hands on the one who invented them.
Some man. A woman wouldn't make anything that ugly.

Out on the stairs, at lunch, in the din of the garage,
She unwraps her sandwich, takes a bite, grimaces.
She thinks of the school girls at their classes
And her friend, still asleep, whose husband works.
Everyone's life is better. Not smart or rich enough
For college, not damned enough to make a good whore.

The afternoon is spent on codes and addresses.
Shipments to Florida, shipments to California.
If she saved she could get her own apartment,
See her mother's face when she moved out of the house.
Worst of all, she thinks she might be pregnant,
And the face of that man makes her want to spit.

AMONG FISHERFOLK

At low tide in the evening along the docks
The net fisherman unloads his catch.
Every night it weighs out less—
More work, less fish, his debt a minus
That rises like water in the bilge
Or deposit bottles stacked on deck.

His debt colors everything he sees—
The green money of the bay, the sun
Setting like an insured boat on fire.
His debt swallows everything to the bottom.

Not long ago this work was glamorous.
Something heroic about the netting of fish.
And girls in halter tops would crowd around
And pictures would be taken of the largest catch.
He would untie his shoes, strip to the waist,
Count three minutes before he'd come up.

THE POINT

Out on the sea at the horizon appears a boat.
It is all there is in the world to think about,
Thinks the man lighting a cigarette with a cupped match.
It is not bound for our port. It has not come out
Of our port. It is going somewhere else. Somewhere else,
That's good, thinks the man, releasing his smoke
      into the willing wind.

THE ROCKPILE

The rockpile stretches out to sea like a series
Of adjacent thoughts—each taking you a little
Farther out—but then there is no conclusion,
Just what you consider the emptiness of the sea.

So it is, of course, the incidents of your life
Have taken you . . . where? One lover piled against
The next, one occupation leaning on another.
Like stubbed cigarettes you have chain-smoked the days.

If the sea had the mind to consider you
On a day when it grew tired of its tides and waves,
It might in its burden envy you—take heart—
And follow you back to your landlocked shore.

EVENING V

There was light in the sky but no twilight.
The south wind battered the trees and houses.
Road signs misinterpreted the highway.
A business caved in—people buried alive.

But you were safe with your tea and whisky,
Watching the storm from your place near the glass,
Recounting like an elder the tribal catastrophes,
Current, previous, last. All this in your robe—
Wrists protruding, fingers stained by smoke.

Where do birds sleep in weather like this?
Dissolve in the rain or enter some fold of the sky?
I think it happened on an evening like this
The prodigal decided it was time.

VOLUME

How is it at a time of joy
The old hurts come back to nibble
Like dogs in a wood, reconsidering
The corpse of a deer. In another room

The beautiful woman sleeps.
Upstairs the child sings as she plays.
Yet once again your sorrow finds you.
Invites itself in to occupy your easy chair.

Sorrow puts its feet up. Sorrow twists
The buttons of your favorite shirt.
It stretches out like fabric, like a rug.
It rests in the slatted dust of Venetian blinds.

When sorrow makes itself at home
The tenants move into corners.
They walk the edges of hallways
And lose their kitchen privileges.

For sorrow dislikes the smell of food,
Especially soups that have cooked all day.
It hates the vegetables cut by hand
And the grains expansive in clear water.

Sorrow feeds on remembered slights.
It listens to only the old tunes.
Sorrow frequents the pick-up joints.
Its favorite color is the faded bruise.

And sorrow maintains the All Night Theatre
In the torn down heart of town,
Where you watch the grainy pictures,
Patrolling the aisles, working the projector.

SPEAKING PARTS

I am an animal
In a topiary garden

Gone to ruin
Try as I will

I cannot determine
The shape I am in

A rhinoceros with a bill
A three humped camel

A great narwhale
In a cloud of krill

Or a lump of stone
The cutter's skill

Graven in the garden
On the hill

RETURN ADDRESS

We shall not go back to the days
When paying the bills was genius,
The ear pressed to the door
Like a risen knot.

Our disembodied figures
Reside there still
Say those who believe
In that room by the sea.

Mourn for the days gone and strange.
Mourn and praise.

INSPIRITER

Why are binoculars often found
Among the possessions of the dead

Have they stood long
Figures in the window
Watching out and over
The sea

While those that have been
At hand have been
Kept at a distance
Seen through the wrong end

Observed like birds of passage
Or planetary movements
In formation and fortune
Auguries rising out of the waves

Foghorn and buoy moan

The skull whistles for its soul

I would be the dog that died for its master

Naked the beloved looks elsewhere

EVENING VI

I am at work here, I am at work there,
Putting both of my best feet forward,
Walking the sidewalks of your city,
Where I linger by the remaining marquees
Behind which you are seated alone,
Or your arm slipped over somebody's
Shoulder. At fifteen I was with you
In the dark, mistaking elbow for breast;
At thirty having sex in the front row.
When is it that we stop being the show?
The film slips and the audience calls "focus."

I follow a woman, I follow the couples,
Through the evening streets of barrels and glass,
Wanting to meet the unmet for supper,
Wanting to know how it is with them.
And nobody asks me about my day.
About the pages in my book of days
Where the thumbed sheets riffled in succession
Propel me like a paper cup.
I know one day I will greet myself
On a street, avenue, or boulevard,
And we will be wearing our black clothes, as planned.

IN CASES LIKE THESE

We do not have a statue or painting of her
And hers were the days before the photograph
Captured so many willing and unwilling subjects.
No portrait of her, though someone must have tried,
Perhaps succeeded, in studio or garret,
North light favoring the contours of her body.
But nothing remains to point her out among
The thousands of unsigned, unidentified works
That clot the halls and basements of public buildings.
Still, it is said (and written) she was beautiful
Of face and body and her voice charmed diplomats
And consorts, and once the King himself raised
A glass in praise of loveliness, a gesture
Which began the usual plottings of Princess
And Priest. Whispers amplified into gossip,
Falsehood translated into sure history.
It did not help that no one knew where
She had come from, how she found her way to court.
In cases like these, the obvious answers
Never matter. How to plead that beauty
Is born anywhere, can have no rank or station,
That beauty should be welcome wherever it goes?
This we know: No one spoke for the accused.
It was easier then than now to let her go.

After the jailors took their turns with her
And the torturer created her new countenance
(sad beneath his mask, one account mentions)
She was released and disappeared forever.
The King grew old. The Princess and her baby
Died in labor. The Duke, her husband, drowned,
Trapped in his armor in a stream. No one knows
What the girl knew of this, or if she survived
Her wounds to live, a hag, huddled in wool,
Begging the outlying huts and far villages.
The courtiers kneeling by the heat of the fire
Would summon the shame of it, an empty kingdom,
Wild folk deployed at the edges of the land,
And beauty desecrated in the basest manner.
Questions rise up. Did the acts of state
Engender its own destruction? Was she, in fact,
A witch or heretic or did she become one
Meting out her own apt forms of vengeance?
Was she then, as now, a persistent illusion?
Catapults knocked down the prized towers.
The Priest died in bed of venereal fever.
Looted tapestries make fine horseblankets.

AN ACCOUNT

"I lived in the city despised by men.
Each night a demon set me to work.
I was given a push broom and shovel
And a large metal barrel on wheels
That were spoked. After Hand Day
I would sweep from the center to the gutter
Of the street, the tumblings and gestures
On the brickwork before the bristles of
My broom like the signings of the deaf
Or the fingertip pressings of the blind.
After Eye Day I was startled by the looks
Of them, rolling on my shovel's blade, each
Seemingly solitary, unpaired, ill at ease.
I could not stand their sight and closed
My own against them. The streets
After Jaw Day were brilliant, the moon
Illuminating the white piles and scatterings
Of teeth, the dried blood at their roots
Reminiscent of soil, the uneven edges
Catching my foot soles. There was nothing
I could do. The maimed and gouged congregated
By the river each morning when I delivered
Their pieces. Always they competed with the beasts
Along the embankment. I recall the footless

Having dragged themselves across the city,
Their clothes' fronts and bodies ribboned,
Consigned to the limbs and mouths of the scavengers.
After Heart Day and Skull Day, I alone waited
To be devoured of my form at nightfall.
The beasts were hungry but they were not cruel.
It was, I suppose, a beautiful thing."

AN ARRANGEMENT

"I looked for something identical to life,
A way of existing without complication—
Not to die, disappear, or become invisible,
But to be present in a different manner.
Still I have trouble describing my life
And my family and friends of former days.
As a child my penmanship was considered poor.
No matter how I practiced the loops and bridges
Of and between the letters would tighten into
An indecipherable thickness. I composed pages
Of sentences on the wide-lined paper, passages
No one else could read. When my teachers
Questioned me, I told them I was a secret agent.
The castles I built on the shore in summer
Were disparaged—their walls not high enough,
Their moats too shallow. But keeping the water
In or out was not my intention. I merely
Constructed my fortress as my hands directed.
My soldier's career might have rounded me out
Better had my sight been clearer. As it was
The targets before me blurred, bull's-eyes
And the shapes of men were formless on the range.
My errors grew larger: inattention and indifference.
The motivated and the monied among us push

The boulders of their days. The years fall
From them, a rain of lemmings from the heights
Until they themselves tumble from the cliff.
My death, I suspect, will be quiet. Something at home
After watching television. There should be nothing more—
Like the set going off forever. Nothing. Like the series
Of zeroes I have peered through, wide-eyed ciphers
One after another, skimming on a lake of infinity,
Saving places for the numerals of greater consequence."

THE EDIFICE

"Filled with myself and hollow
As the bronze cast of a statue,
I lived within the figure of myself
And the one always the world
Provided. Like a comedian
And a gangster, I stood up
To the mirror where I tested
My impressions, trying to appear
Natural, as it were, and cool.
You can imagine things I might
Have done, kung fu kicks, nude
Yoga, posings like the martyr,
The overhead light washing me in dust.
And you can imagine things I might
Have said, whispered to the pleasure
Of my own ear, my expectant face
Ballooning with possibility, reliable
As a parrot about to repeat
Its bright word, 'hello,' measured
By degrees through all its ardent
Ranges, the young man's gambit
Transformed to the Cockney huckster.
When I consider my appearance
I envision a foreign city at night,

The still, illuminated monuments
Aging where they stand. Beneath
Their stones, the whiff of urine,
Of death, altar upon altar,
Flesh on flesh, our slow dispersals
Into the earth. I can show you
To the places where love has gone awry
In its temporal and corporeal forms."

GATES OF THE CITY

Out, after work, in summer, on the avenues,
The corporate employees walk home in linen clothes.

It is Friday and they have begun
To grow their bodies again.

And the one who was just a mouth
Has eyes, a nose, a brow.

And the one whose hand refused a loan claps hands.
And the seated one rises, smooths its pants.

And the one who was promoted goes to supper.
And the one who was dull is a bore.

And the one who must hurry will sleep by the ocean.
And the one on fire will drink on a porch in the rain.

I watch them at their changes on my way home,
Believing in what it is that next they will become.

EVENING VII

Whose doorbell did I press, what chime
Played out the notes of another house
I entered what should not be long ago but is,
Whose voice through the woodwork asked
Who's there, what did those tones suggest,
The plush rug, my mirrored face in the hall,
A cooking aroma still unresolved, hanging
In the air like a sweet cloud, a little
Vacant now but palpable as hands remembering
Hands, as hands extending into the air?

That skin felt real, can still be held
The way what remains in time gets held
A fixed embrace, naked as the one
Beneath the wrappings of husband and wife
Fitted together in their double sarcophagus,
Sailing on a pallet through the royal night
Down the fabled river, where the owls
Break in standing timber, and what remains
Of a soul gets haunted by flesh, their
Continuous movement disguised as rest.

House of the past, that living room
Spawned fancies and migrations, the great
Passage of the day, the twilit century
Undraped, seen through the picture window,
The sun, a scribe, accountable and true
To the spirits of our evenings and avenues.

The sea is far from home now. The sea is
Somewhere I can get through this door and out
Another, through the yards and trees and over
The wall, if she were there to let me in.

PSALM

When the dove of whom there is no memory fell into the sea
We were uncreated, oh yeah, we were speechless before the sky.
There were no words to be sung on the water without edges.
Lord had shown his preference for his serpents and his mosses.

Into depths we drowned, the familial and the animal,
Paired on the deck of our craft going round.
Into depths we drowned and we were lost among us . . .
The opened cages, our bodies starving in the sun.

SEVERAL DIORAMAS,
SOME REMEMBERED,
SOME INVENTED,
FROM THE MUSÉE GREVIN

Napoleon appears so lonely on his island
The painted sea and sky on the floor and wall
Behind him convey to the viewer great tragedy.
The fierceness in the little man's eyes
Below the edge of his three-cornered hat
Evokes the woundedness of the truly misunderstood.

The victories at Iena and Austerlitz
The coronation at Notre Dame
The woman and the pond swan
He will never see again
From the window at Malmaison.

The royal children in their servant's chamber,
Gold concealed beneath girdles and britches,
Tempt us to weep at their ill fortune—
As from the dull notes on the hidden speaker
The drop chop of the guillotine is not an imagined
Rhythm of their final deprivation.

The Sun King is displeased.
He worries for his steeds' steeds' steeds;
Sitting on a golden throne
In the formal garden
He has made a Versailles of Heaven.

And here is the waxworks of childhood fear.
A man and a woman face separate directions.
They look cold and rigid as polished columns.
The child in the arch tries to pull them together,
(Or are they pulling him apart, is that the situation?)
St. Hippolytus with a more familiar resemblance.

Now that we have borne witness
To the slaughter of the innocents
We may leave this darkened cellar.
Hold tight the handrail
Upstairs we walk upon the moon.

Stuart Dischell was born in Atlantic City, New Jersey. *Good Hope Road*, his first book, was a 1991 National Poetry Series selection. His poems have appeared in many publications, including *AGNI*, *The New Republic*, *Partisan Review*, and *Ploughshares*. He has been awarded the Pushcart Prize and is the recipient of a 1996 National Endowment for the Arts Fellowship in Literature. Dischell has been on the English faculty at Boston University and New Mexico State University. He now teaches in the Master of Fine Arts program at the University of North Carolina at Greensboro.

PENGUIN POETS

Paul Beatty	*Joker, Joker, Deuce*
Ted Berrigan	*Selected Poems*
Philip Booth	*Pairs*
Jim Carroll	*Fear of Dreaming*
Nicholas Christopher	*5° & Other Poems*
Stuart Dischell	*Evenings & Avenues*
Stephen Dobyns	*Common Carnage*
Paul Durcan	*A Snail in My Prime*
Amy Gerstler	*Nerve Storm*
Debora Greger	*Desert Fathers, Uranium Daughters*
Robert Hunter	*Sentinel*
Jack Kerouac	*Book of Blues*
Ann Lauterbach	*And For Example*
Derek Mahon	*Selected Poems*
Michael McClure	*Three Poems*
Alice Notley	*The Descent of Alette*
Anne Waldman	*Kill or Cure*
Robert Wrigley	*In the Bank of Beautiful Sins*